Puppy

Spellbound at School

SUE BENTLEY

Illustrated by Angela Swan

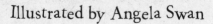

Grosset & Dunlap
An Imprint of Penguin Group (USA) LLC

Magic Puppy

To Rex—an early companion, strong and loyal

GROSSET & DUNLAP
Published by the Penguin Group
Penguin Group (USA) LLC, 375 Hudson Street, New York, New York 10014, USA

USA | Canada | UK | Ireland | Australia | New Zealand | India | South Africa | China

penguin.com
A Penguin Random House Company

Text copyright © 2009 Sue Bentley. Illustrations copyright © 2009 Angela Swan. Cover illustration © 2009 Andrew Farley. First printed in Great Britain in 2009 by Penguin Books Ltd. First published in the United States in 2014 by Grosset & Dunlap, a division of Penguin Young Readers Group, 345 Hudson Street, New York, New York 10014. GROSSET & DUNLAP is a trademark of Penguin Group (USA) LLC. Printed in the U.S.A.

Library of Congress Cataloging-in-Publication Data is available.

ISBN 978-0-448-46790-0   10 9 8 7 6 5 4 3 2 1

Prologue

The young silver-gray wolf leaped across the freezing water, jumping between huge slabs of floating ice. Storm paused and lifted his head up to the cold light of the moon. It felt good to be back.

Suddenly a terrifying howl rang out in the night air. Storm froze.

"Shadow!" he gasped.

The cruel lone wolf who had attacked

Storm's Moon-claw pack was very close.

There was a dazzling flash of bright gold light and a silent explosion of sparks. Where the young silver-gray wolf had been standing, there now crouched a tiny shih tzu puppy with fluffy black-and-white fur, a flattish face with a button nose, short legs, and bright midnight blue eyes.

Storm whined softly. He should have known it wasn't safe. He hoped that this disguise would protect him.

His puppy heart beat fast as he looked around nervously for somewhere safe to hide. As far as the eye could see there was only treacherous dark water and huge floating slabs of ice.

Storm tensed as he spotted a wolf speeding toward him. It was running and jumping like the wind, despite using only three of its legs.

"Mother!" Storm leaped forward and tore across the ice floes toward her. The injured she-wolf stopped and bent her head as the tiny puppy ran up to her. Storm's whole body wriggled and his little high-set tail twirled as he licked her muzzle in greeting.

"I am glad to see you again, my son," Canista panted, her gray sides heaving. "But you cannot stay. Shadow is not far behind me."

Storm raised his head and saw a tiny dot out on the ice, growing bigger with every passing second as it got closer. His midnight blue eyes glinted with anger and fear. "Let us fight him now and force him to leave our land forever!"

Canista's tired, gentle face flickered with pride. "He is too strong for you to face alone, and I am weak from his poisoned bite and cannot help you. Use this disguise and hide in the other world. Return when you are wiser and your magic is stronger."

Storm nodded slowly. He knew that his mother was right, but he hated to leave her. Leaning close, he huffed out a glittering puppy breath that swirled around Canista's injured leg for a few seconds before disappearing into her fur.

"Thank you, Storm. I feel a little stronger," Canista rumbled softly.

Another powerful howl split the silence. Shadow was close now. Outlined against the starlit sky, he crouched, ready to spring.

Gold sparks ignited in the tiny puppy's fluffy black-and-white fur. Storm whimpered as he felt the power building inside him. The gold glow around him grew brighter. And brighter . . .

Chapter
ONE

Lola Evans propped her chin in her hands, idly watching the dragon shape in the cottony clouds in the sky outside the classroom window.

Ms. Dobson was speaking. "Now class, we're going to learn about recycling today. Are you listening, Lola?"

Lola jumped and felt herself going hot at being caught daydreaming. "Sorry, ma'am. Um . . . will we have to go around collecting garbage and stuff?" she asked.

Carly, who sat at a desk next to Lola, glanced across at her. "That shouldn't be a problem for you. My mom says the neighborhood where you live looks like a big junkyard," she whispered so that only Lola heard.

Lola ignored her, but her cheeks burned even more.

Carly lived in a big house on a leafy avenue. She was the most popular girl in class and nearly always got good grades on her school projects. Today she wore glittery pink barrettes in her straight blond hair.

Ms. Dobson smiled. "Good question, Lola. But there's a lot more to it than that. It's about not wasting things and thinking

of interesting ways to reuse them."

"My mom's great at recycling stuff,"
Lola said, starting to get interested. This
topic sounded like it might turn out to be
fun. She knew a bit about it already, and
she thought she might even be quite good
at it. "She saves wrapping paper to use
again and puts plastic bottles and cans out
for the weekly collection."

"Duh! Everyone does that!" Carly
scoffed. "I know, ma'am! I'm going to

recycle my old Barbie dolls by giving
them to the kids' hospital!"

"That's a wonderful idea. Very good,
Carly!" Everyone began talking at once
about different ways of recycling, and
Ms. Dobson held up a hand for silence.
"Hold your horses, everyone. To get you
all motivated, I'm going to make this
into a competition. There'll be a prize for
the winners. Movie tickets for the latest
summer blockbuster! You'll be working in
groups, so I want you to get into teams
of three."

There was a scraping of chairs and
then a frantic scramble as friends hurried
around and joined teams. Lola went
toward one group, but there were already
three kids in it. She turned round and
almost bumped into Carly and Treena

Cox, a tall, thin girl with glasses.

"Don't even *think* about it!" Carly warned, the braces on her teeth glinting. "Lee! Quick, come over here with me and Treena. I want the best team." She waved to a stocky boy with spiky hair.

"I wouldn't be in *your* team if you paid me!" Lola murmured to herself, trying not to show that she was hurt.

Looking around the class, she saw that everyone else had teamed up. Her shoulders drooped. It looked like she was going to be left on her own, but then she saw Ms. Dobson coming toward her with Jaidon Brooks.

Jaidon was a quiet boy with longish, curly dark-blond hair, who had only joined the class last quarter. Lola had tried to speak to him a couple of times, but he

hadn't seemed like he wanted to make
friends with her or anyone else. And, right
now, he stood there making circles on the
floor with the toe of one shoe.

"Lola!" said Ms. Dobson. "You and
Jaidon seem to be at a loose ends. I
thought you could team up together."

"But that means there are only two of
us in our team!" Lola protested. *And Jaidon*

hardly ever says anything, anyway, so I'm really just a team of one!

"You're a resourceful girl, Lola. I'm sure you're capable of making a special effort." The teacher unrolled a wall chart and wrote Lola's and Jaidon's names, and then added a number ten in the column beneath. "There. These points will give you a head start."

Everyone crowded around as the teacher filled in the team names on the wall chart. It was almost time to go home, but Ms. Dobson had one more thing to say.

"Have a good weekend. And on Monday, I want you all to bring some things from home to put on our display table. Good luck with the competition!"

The bell rang for the end of class, and everyone filed out.

Lola and Jaidon wandered into the playground together in silence. Deciding to try to make the best of things, Lola smiled at him. "So we're teammates, then. It'd be great if we could win this with just two of us. Don't you think?"

Jaidon didn't look at her. He shrugged. "I . . . um . . . guess so."

They reached the school gates, where Carly, Treena, and Lee were discussing what they were going to bring to school on Monday. "How about some Styrofoam to-go containers . . . ," Lee was saying.

"Shhh!" Treena eyed Jaidon and Lola through her glasses. "We don't want to give *them* any ideas."

"We've got lots of ideas of our own, thanks," Lola said.

"Really?" Carly sang out. "Well, here's another: Why don't I recycle some of my old dresses by giving them to you? Then maybe you won't have to run around after school in scruffy jeans and a T-shirt all the time!"

Treena and Lee snickered.

Lola prickled with indignation. "No, thanks. I like my jeans, and, anyway, I don't feel like dressing up like a pathetic stick of cotton candy!" she shot back spiritedly.

Treena nudged Carly. "I'll have your old stuff, if you're giving it away."

"Oh, shut up," Carly said irritably, obviously annoyed that Lola seemed to have gotten the upper hand for once.

Lola looked around to grin triumphantly at Jaidon and noticed that he was backing away nervously. "Um . . .

Gotta go. See you at school on Monday," he mumbled.

"Hey, wait! What about our stuff for the display table . . . ?" Lola called after him, but Jaidon was already jogging away down the street.

"Great!" Lola murmured, as she started walking home by herself. She got the

feeling she'd be doing this project all on
her own.

A few minutes later, Lola turned
onto her street. There were some older
kids kicking a soccer ball against a row
of shabby garages. Another boy was
skateboarding down the sidewalk, avoiding
the cracks where weeds pushed through.
They all shouted "hello" to Lola, and
she waved back as she went into the
apartment building where she lived.

Her mom and dad didn't get home for
another two hours, so Lola usually went to
her neighbor's apartment and played with
her little kids. But today she wasn't in the
mood. She popped next door, just to say
that she was home, and then wandered
into the kitchen to get herself a snack.

As she opened a cabinet, Lola was

suddenly blinded by a dazzling flash of
bright gold light.

"Oh!" she gasped, taking a step back.
Lola rubbed her eyes and looked up to see
a tiny, fluffy black-and-white puppy, with
a cute, flattish face, a button nose, short
legs, and enormous midnight blue eyes
glowing from under a tiny fringe. It was
staring at her from where it sat on a shelf,
next to some cans of baked beans.

"Can you help me, please?" it woofed.

Chapter
TWO

Lola stared at the tiny puppy in complete astonishment. "Wha-what . . . er . . . I mean, who are you?" she stammered, not quite able to believe what was happening.

"I am Storm of the Moon-claw pack. I have just arrived here from far away," the puppy yapped, looking at her with an intelligent expression.

Lola's eyes widened in shock. "You

really can talk!" she gasped.

"Yes, all of my pack can." Storm sat
there with his ears pricked. "What is your
name?"

"I'm L-Lola Evans," Lola found herself
spluttering. "I . . . live here with . . . with
my . . . mom and dad."

She took another step backward, so as
not to alarm this amazing puppy. She still
couldn't quite believe this was happening
and she didn't want Storm to jump down

from the high shelf and hurt himself while trying to get away.

Storm dipped his little black-and-white head. "I am honored to meet you, Lola."

"Um . . . me too." Lola blinked as she remembered something that Storm had said. "Why do you need my help?"

Storm's midnight blue eyes flashed with anger. "My mother and father were the leaders of our Moon-claw pack. But a fierce lone wolf called Shadow attacked us. He killed my father and three litter brothers and left my mother injured. Now he wants to lead the pack, but the others will not follow Shadow while I am alive."

"Just a minute. Did you say wolf? But you're a tiny pu--"

"Please stand back," Storm ordered, leaping down from the shelf in a glittering

fountain of gold sparks and landing softly
on the floor behind Lola.

As Lola whipped around toward him,
there was another blinding flash that lit
up the entire kitchen this time.

"Oh!" Lola rubbed her eyes and
blinked hard. To her amazement, she saw
that the tiny black-and-white puppy had
gone, and in its place stood a magnificent
young silver-gray wolf with thick fur and
huge velvety paws that seemed too big
for his body. Despite being young, he had
large, sharp teeth and a thick neck-ruff
that glittered with big golden sparkles.

Lola backed away warily. "Storm,
is . . . is that still you?"

"Yes, Lola. Do not be afraid. I will
not harm you," Storm told her in a deep,
gentle growl.

But before Lola had time to get used to the sight of the majestic young wolf standing in the middle of her kitchen, there was a final gold flash and Storm reappeared as a tiny, helpless puppy.

"Whoa! That's some disguise!" Lola exclaimed, deeply impressed.

Storm crouched down, so that his fluffy tummy brushed the floor and she saw that his tiny black-and-white body was beginning to tremble all over.

"It will not save me if Shadow uses his magic to find me. I need to hide now. Can you help?" he whined.

Lola's heart went out to the little puppy who was all alone and trying to make the best of things in any way he could. Right now, Lola felt a bit like that herself.

She picked up Storm. As she stroked
his soft little head, his fringe tickled her
fingers. "Of course I'll help you. You can
stay here with m——" She stopped as she
remembered her parents' strict rules about
having pets.

"Oh, I don't know if I can keep you.
We're all out all day, and Mom and Dad
don't think it's fair to leave a pet by itself."

"I understand, Lola. Thank you for your kindness. I will leave now and find someone else who can help me."

"Oh, please wait!" Lola said urgently. She wasn't ready to lose him just yet. Before he'd arrived she'd been feeling so lonely and fed up. Because of Carly's mean comments, not many of Lola's classmates were brave enough to be her friend. Jaidon didn't exactly say much, either.

"There must be some way I can keep you here. Maybe I could hide you in my bedroom. But it would be really boring for you to have to stay at home and be quiet all the time," she said thoughtfully.

"I would like to stay here with you!" Storm looked up at her with eager midnight blue eyes. "And I can use my

magic so that only you will be able to see
and hear me."

"Really? You can make yourself
invisible?" Lola said. "Then I don't need to
worry about hiding you from Mom and
Dad. Oooh! You can even sleep on my bed."

Storm grinned, showing his sharp little
puppy teeth. "Thank you, Lola," he woofed.
He leaned up and licked the end of her
nose with his wet pink tongue.

Lola smiled down at the adorable puppy.
She felt her heart lighten as she cuddled
Storm's sturdy little body. "Even Jaidon
will be excited when I tell him about you.
Maybe he'll even want to be friends . . ."

Storm stiffened and his cute little
squashed face became very serious. "You
cannot tell anyone my secret. Promise
me, Lola."

"Oh. Really? Well, okay, then." It would have been nice to have something to break the ice with Jaidon. But Lola didn't want to put Storm in danger, so she was prepared to agree. "Cross my heart. No one's going to hear about you from me!"

"Thank you, Lola."

Lola gently rubbed one of the puppy's tiny ears between her finger and thumb. "I bet you're hungry after your long journey, aren't you?"

Storm nodded and wagged his tail. The little tail, set high on his rump, looked just like a tiny black-and-white mop! Lola hid a smile, not wanting to hurt Storm's feelings. She bent down and put him on the floor, before reaching up for a can of tuna.

As soon as Lola had forked the fish on

to a saucer and put it on the floor, Storm
began chomping it up. He finished it in
a few gulps and then sat down to lick his
chops.

"Delicious!"

"I'm sorry we don't have any dog food," Lola apologized. She had a sudden thought. "I still have some of last week's allowance money left. Let's go out to the store and get you some."

Woof! Storm immediately leaped to his feet and danced about excitedly on his short legs. "And shall we go for a walk, too?"

"You bet! There's plenty of time before Mom and Dad get home. But I think you'd better make yourself invisible, just in case anyone I know sees me with you."

Lola felt a faint tingling sensation down her spine and a few gold sparks fizzed out of the ends of Storm's floppy little triangular ears. "It is done!" he yapped.

As Lola went outside with the playful

pup, she felt her spirits beginning to rise.
She might not wear cool clothes like
Carly or be in the popular group, but she
had something really special—a secret
furry friend.

Chapter
THREE

Lola woke early the following Monday morning, feeling rather hot. She put her hands up to push away her comforter and found that she seemed to be wearing a fluffy scarf, which was snoring very softly.

Storm! Lola grinned. She stroked the sleeping puppy, who was draped across her chest with his little head tucked up close under her chin.

Storm lifted his head and yawned.

"Pew!" Lola said, giggling as she fanned away a warm blast of fishy puppy breath. "Did you sleep well?"

"Yes I did. I like it here. It is a safe place," Storm woofed happily.

Lola gave him a cuddle. "Good. Because I love having you living with me, too! This weekend has been great."

Lola gently moved Storm aside before throwing back the comforter and putting on her school uniform. She fed the tiny puppy and then washed his food bowl and hid it in the bottom of her wardrobe with his cans of food, before going to get her breakfast.

Storm scampered into the kitchen beside her and then curled up invisibly on Lola's lap while she ate. Lola smiled

to herself as she looked across the table
at her mom and dad. She imagined the
looks on their faces if she told them that a
magic puppy was sitting only a foot away!

Fifteen minutes later, Lola put her
book bag by the front door. She popped
her head into the kitchen. "Bye, Mom.
Bye, Dad. See you later."

"Bye, honey," her dad called.

Her mom smiled. "Have a good day at school!"

Lola turned back into the hall to see that Storm had jumped into her open bag. He was sitting next to her books, with an eager expression on his face.

"I am ready!"

Lola laughed delightedly. "I'd love you to come to school. But you'll have to keep out of Ms. Dobson's way. She's our teacher, and she's quite strict."

Storm's midnight blue eyes twinkled. "I promise."

The sinking feeling that Lola usually felt at the thought of another day of Carly's teasing suddenly didn't seem quite so bad as she made her way to school with Storm peering out of her bag. Lola held her book bag steady as she walked into

the classroom. Storm sat with his paws
looped over the top of the bag. His black
button nose twitched as he snuffed up the
interesting smells all around him.

Even though he was invisible, Lola
was still a bit nervous about the teacher
or one of her classmates noticing the tiny
puppy. But when no one paid Storm any
attention, she felt herself starting to relax.

Once the class was settled at their

desks, Ms. Dobson took attendance. Lola noticed that when the teacher called Jaidon's name, there was no answer, and his seat at the nearby desk was still empty.

Storm jumped out of her bag and went off to explore the room. Lola smiled to herself as she watched his sturdy little form snuffling about under the desks and poking inquiringly into other open school bags.

Ms. Dobson put the register away and looked up. "Has everyone brought something for the display table?"

"I have!" Carly jumped to her feet, holding a cereal box. She went straight over and put it on the display table.

"That's a great start, Carly," Ms. Dobson praised. "You get one point for your team. Recycling cardboard and paper packaging means fewer trees need to be cut down."

Looking pleased with herself, Carly took her seat again.

Other kids were producing plastic food trays, tinfoil, and all kinds of packaging. The display table began to fill up, and Ms. Dobson doled out more team points. Kids went forward and crowded around to study the wall chart and see who'd been awarded the most points.

Lola would normally have been up there with the other kids, but she was watching out for Storm, who was nosing into an open floor cupboard. He suddenly leaped sideways as the door swung open and an avalanche of paper spilled out onto the floor.

A girl standing nearby frowned in
puzzlement. "How did that happen?" she
said, bending down to put the paper back
into the cupboard.

Lola had just reassured herself that
Storm was unharmed when Carly called
out in a loud voice: "What did *you* bring,
Lola?"

Lola nearly jumped out of her skin.
She suddenly realized that with the

excitement of finding Storm, she had
forgotten to bring anything for the display
table. She slid down in her seat and
pretended that she hadn't heard.

But Carly wasn't going to be put off.
"I said—WHAT DID *YOU* BRING,
LOLA?"

Lola rolled her eyes. "If you must
know, I . . . er . . . didn't have time to . . ."

"She forgot! What a dummy!" Carly
hooted, with a smug grin.

Ms. Dobson glanced at Lola with
raised eyebrows. "It's a pretty poor
showing. I'm afraid you're going to have
to make a bit more of an effort if you
want to win the prize."

"Yes, ma'am," Lola said quietly.

A few moments later, Storm padded
across the classroom. He jumped straight

up in a whoosh of tiny sparks to sit on Lola's desk. She made sure that no one was looking before she reached out and stroked him.

The tiny puppy tilted his head and blinked at her with bright eyes. "Is something wrong, Lola?"

Lola sighed and nodded her head slowly. "It's no big deal. It was my fault for forgetting to bring something for our project. But Carly deliberately made a big fuss about it, so I got into trouble with Ms. Dobson."

"Who is Carly?" Storm yapped.

"That's her over there." Lola pointed toward the other girl, who had just sat back down at her own desk. She was slowly running her special purple brush through her long blond hair.

Lola didn't notice the thoughtful look
on Storm's face because, at that moment,
the classroom door opened and Jaidon
rushed in, looking hot and flustered.

Chapter
FOUR

"Sorry, I'm . . . um . . . late, ma'am,"
Jaidon murmured. "Dad's van broke
down—again."

Ms. Dobson nodded. "All right. But
this is the third time you've been late in a
month. If it happens again, I'll need you to
bring me a letter from home."

Jaidon flushed bright red. "Yes, ma'am.
Sorry," he mumbled again, pushing back

his damp curly hair.

"I feel bad for him—he couldn't help being late," Lola whispered to Storm as Jaidon walked toward her on his way to his own desk. "I know how horrible it is when the whole class is looking at you."

"Hi, Jaidon," she called, smiling, to try to make him feel a bit better.

Jaidon looked surprised. But Lola was delighted when she was rewarded with a shy grin back. "Hi, Lola. I've . . . er . . . brought this for the display table." Taking something out of his school bag, he shoved it across the desk toward her.

It was a pen-holder made out of a cut-up plastic soda bottle, decorated with colorful swirls of acrylic paint.

"Wow! That's really good!" Lola said, her eyes widening. "Where did you get it?

"I made it last night. Should we put
it on the table with the other stuff?"

"You bet!" Lola jumped to her feet,
pleased that Jaidon was turning out to be
quite a good partner! Storm leaped down
from the desk and padded after them.

Carly got up, too, and zoomed back
toward the table to see what was going on.
The kids who were still there moved aside

as Jaidon put the pen-holder with the other stuff.

Ms. Dobson leaned over to look at it. "That's very inventive: a fine example of recycling something old into something new. Double points to Lola and Jaidon's team!"

"Double points? That's not fair," Carly complained.

Lola felt like jumping up and down with joy, but Storm was standing close to her ankles and she didn't want to step on him. She was wondering how to warn him to stay under the table, without attracting attention, when Carly impatiently elbowed her aside.

"Let me see that pen-holder!" Carly demanded, accidentally stepping on one of Storm's paws.

Yipe! Yipe! Storm yelped in pain.

"Watch out!" Lola warned, giving Carly a gentle nudge, so that she'd shift over and release Storm's paw.

"Oh!" Carly cried. She flung up both arms and spun around dramatically. Pretending to lose her balance, she sprawled right across the table. Paper, cardboard, and plastic went flying and bounced on to the floor.

Ms. Dobson looked up and her eyebrows knitted in a frown. "Whatever's going on over there?"

"Lola pushed me over!" Carly accused. "I didn't do anything to her. She's just jealous because I've got a top team, and she's stuck with wimpy old Jaidon!"

"I hardly touched her! She stepped on my friend's . . ." Lola stopped as she

realized that she couldn't explain without
mentioning Storm. "On my foot. I was
just trying to get her to move."

Ms. Dobson looked at Carly. "Is this
true?"

"No! She deliberately pushed me—really hard!" Carly fibbed. Lola opened her mouth to speak and then changed her mind. What was the point? Everyone was going to believe Carly.

"I saw what happened," Jaidon said unexpectedly. "Lola only gave her a gentle nudge. Carly made it look much worse than it was."

Lola looked at Jaidon in surprise. It was the most she had ever heard him say at one time. She smiled gratefully at him.

"It sounds to me like this was a storm in a teacup," Ms. Dobson said. "We'll say no more about it. Can we all clean up this mess, please? And then will you get out your workbooks?"

Everyone began picking things up.

While no one was looking, Lola quickly bent down to check that Storm wasn't hurt. "How's your paw? Is it sore?" she whispered to him.

"My paw is already starting to feel better now," he woofed, wagging his tail.

Once the display table was neat and tidy, kids began to file back to their desks and start work.

Carly paused to smirk at Lola and Jaidon on her way back to her desk. "You might have gotten out of trouble this time, but I'm going to win this competition. You just see if I don't!" Plonking herself down in her seat, she took out her shiny pink metal pencil case.

Storm frowned. Lola felt a faint tingling feeling down her spine and gasped as she saw gold sparkles blooming

in his black-and-white fur. What was
happening? Suddenly Carly's pencil case
unclipped itself and all her pencils, pens,
and felt tips sprayed into the air.

"Eek!" Carly shrieked in surprise,
ducking as they bounced onto her desk
with a loud rattling noise.

"Stop messing around, Carly!" Ms.
Dobson said crossly. "I don't know what's
gotten into you today!"

Lola tried not laugh. "Storm! That was naughty! But actually it did serve her right."

Carly gathered up her pens in moody silence.

Lola really enjoyed having Storm with her at school the following day. She always liked Tuesdays. They had gym in the mornings and then reading in the afternoon—her two favorite things. The day seemed to fly by.

As the bell rang for the end of the day, Lola stacked her books in her bag and then made room for Storm to jump inside. "See you tomorrow," she called to Jaidon on her way out of the classroom. "Unless you . . . um . . . feel like walking home with me," she said as a sudden afterthought.

"I live too far away to walk, right across town," Jaidon told her. "My dad's picking me up."

At first, Lola wondered if Jaidon had found out that she lived in the messy, rundown neighborhood and didn't want to go home that way. But then she decided that he didn't seem like that sort of boy. The last couple of days, he had really come out of his shell, and it had been nice to have someone to talk to—even if it had been mainly about the project. Lola had decided that Jaidon just must have been a bit shy.

"Where's your house, then?" she asked, thinking that maybe he lived in one of the big houses near Carly.

"It's . . . er . . . not exactly a house. We live in . . . a place you wouldn't have

heard of!" Jaidon shot away out of the
school gates. "See you!"

Lola raised her eyebrows. "I don't get
it," she whispered to Storm. "One minute
I think Jaidon's starting to be friendlier,
and the next he's running off again."

They had turned the corner now and
were out of sight of school. Just in case
anyone was looking, Lola pretended to
fiddle about with her school books as she
put her bag down so that Storm could
jump out.

He shook himself and then trotted
beside her down the street. "I think Jaidon
is a kind boy," he woofed decisively.
"Perhaps there is some reason for the way
he is."

Lola hadn't thought of that. She
wondered if the magic puppy might be

right. Storm stopped to sniff the wall of a store. Lola paused to wait for him. There were some unusual metal lanterns with lacy cut-out shapes in the window display. "Those are pretty. It's Mom's birthday soon. I'd love to buy her one of those."

Storm reared up on to his back legs and put his front paws on the glass to

look in the store window. Lola smiled, feeling a rush of affection for her tiny friend. Sometimes it was hard to believe that Storm was really a wild and powerful young wolf. She bent down to stroke the puppy's fluffy black-and-white fur. "Let's go. No point looking at things I'd have to save for a whole year to be able to buy."

Chapter
FIVE

The display table was filling up with interesting things. There were bookmarks and gift tags made from used greeting cards. Carly had glued matchboxes together into a tiny chest, decorated with pink glitter and stars, for keeping her hair barrettes in.

Even Lola had to admit it looked pretty cool and was worth the extra team points it earned for Carly's team. As expected, Carly, Treena, and Lee were now way ahead of everyone else on the wall chart.

Lola racked her brain, trying to think of something different that she could make or recycle. After all, Jaidon had come up with the pen-holder, so it was her turn. "I just can't think of anything that someone hasn't already done," she whispered glumly to Storm. "And we really need to earn some more points."

"I have noticed that human food comes in lots of different containers," Storm observed. "Perhaps you could use one of those?"

"But which one . . . ?" Lola paused, as a half-formed idea rose into her head. "Yogurt cups! Everyone has tons of those. Maybe we could make something from them. I'll tell Jaidon at recess. Thanks, Storm!"

Storm's bright blue eyes twinkled happily. "You are welcome."

But when Lola told Jaidon, he shook his head. "We don't buy yogurt in plastic cups. Mom makes it in a dish with milk from our cows—" He stopped as he saw Lola looking curiously at him. "I didn't mean to tell you that. Now you probably think I'm weird or something."

"No, I don't. It sounds great. I don't

know anyone who makes their own yogurt! I'd love to try some," Lola said.

"Really?" Jaidon said, as if he didn't quite believe her.

"Really," Lola repeated. "So, do you live on a farm?"

"Sort of. We grow our own vegetables and sell them and stuff," Jaidon said. He chewed his lip and seemed to be making up his mind to tell her something. He took a deep breath. "I don't really like to talk about where I live, because the kids in my old school used to make fun of me when they found out."

Just like Carly and her friends do with me, Lola thought. "That's so mean. I can't stand kids like that!" she said.

"Me, neither," Jaidon said, his shy smile broadening.

Lola wondered if Jaidon might tell
her more. But as Carly, Treena, and Lee
drifted over, laughing and chattering
among themselves, Jaidon clammed up
again.

"It must be great to grow your own
food and keep animals, like Jaidon's mom
and dad," Lola commented to Storm,
before dinner that evening. "But I don't
blame him for not talking to anyone
about where he lives, especially after what
happened at his old school."

Storm nodded, his midnight blue
eyes gleaming with sympathy. "I think he
might eventually tell someone he thinks
he can trust."

"Do you really think so?" Lola asked.

"Yes, Lola! Or maybe someone

who can keep a really big secret," Storm woofed, his tail twirling.

"Like me?" Lola laughed. She threw her arms round her wise little friend and gave him an affectionate cuddle. "You're the best secret in the whole universe, and you're all mine!"

After they ate dinner, Lola helped her mom clean up, and then she went into her bedroom with Storm. "I'm going to read for a while and maybe work on my school project," she told her parents.

Her mom smiled. "All right, honey. I'll come in and say good night later."

Lola had only managed to slip a few treats to Storm during supper, so she fed him some more in her bedroom. After he finished eating, Storm padded after her as she slipped quietly into the kitchen to

wash out the empty dog-food can and
hide it in the recycling bin outside the
back door.

"I still can't decide what to take
to school tomorrow. My mind's gone
completely blank," she said with a groan.
"I might as well face it—Carly's team's
going to win this competition, hands
down."

Storm's bright blue eyes lit up. "Put
the empty can on the floor, please!" Lola
was puzzled but she did as he asked. She
felt a warm tingling sensation down her
spine as gold sparks bloomed in Storm's
black-and-white fur and his ears and tail
fizzled with magical power. He pointed
one tiny front paw and a fountain of
shimmering sparks shot out and swirled
around the empty can.

As Lola watched in amazement,
streams of tiny sparks like miniature laser
beams pinged up and down, polishing the
can and punching out a pattern of holes in
a pretty design. There was a final flash and
crackling noise, and the glittery work was
done.

"Wow!" Lola picked up the can,
which had been magically transformed
into a tiny lantern, complete with looped

handle and folded-over sharp edges.
"This is perfect. It's like the ones we
saw in that fancy store, only much nicer.
No one else will think of this. You're
amazing! Thanks, Storm." She grinned
at him, wide-eyed. "Would it be too
much to ask you to make a couple more?
Then I can give them to Mom for her
birthday."

Storm's little muzzle wrinkled in a
smile. "I would be delighted to do that!
You are welcome."

The can lantern was a massive hit with
everyone in class when Lola placed it on
the display table the next morning. Even
Ms. Dobson was impressed. "Well done,
Lola. That's really inventive."

"Yeah! It's awesome!" Jaidon enthused,

forgetting to be shy for once. "So much better than my pen-holder!"

Lola beamed at Storm, who was sitting invisibly on her desk. She really wished that she could tell everyone that he was the one who made it.

"Lola couldn't have made that lantern by herself. She's a cheat!" said an accusing voice.

Lola didn't need to look around to see who was speaking. She sighed. On this occasion, Carly was right. She'd had help and couldn't deny it, and if Ms. Dobson agreed with Carly, she and Jaidon were about to lose points!

But an amazing thing happened.

"It's sensible to get an adult to help sometimes, if you're making something complicated," the teacher decided. "I'm

going to give Lola and Jaidon's team extra
points for showing initiative."

"Yay!" Lola did a little dance of
triumph and Jaidon laughed. "Look!"
she told him. "We're neck and neck with
Carly, Treena, and Lee! We have a good
chance of winning!"

"I wouldn't bet on it! You'll have to
come up with something outstanding to
beat me!" Carly boasted, overhearing.

Jaidon glanced at Lola, the light of battle in his eyes. "That sounds like a challenge to me. What do you think?"

"I'm up for it if you are!" Lola said.

Chapter
SIX

Ms. Dobson announced some exciting news at the beginning of the following week.

"As part of our project, we're taking a field trip to the local recycling center."

"Sounds like fun!" Lola whispered to Storm. "I love school trips."

Gru-uff! Storm agreed.

At recess, Lola took Storm for a

walk across the playing field. He ran around, happily chasing a butterfly, before throwing himself on to his back and rolling around with all four short legs in the air.

Lola looked up from watching Storm's funny antics to see Jaidon approaching. He looked like he had something on his mind.

"Hi," Jaidon said, shuffling his feet. He swallowed and went a bit red. "I was thinking, I mean, I . . . um . . . wondered if you'd like to come over my house sometime? I'll understand if you don't want to . . ."

"No! I mean, yes, I'd love to!" Lola hid her surprise. Jaidon Brooks was inviting *her* to *his* house? "Maybe we could write up our notes together after Friday's trip to the recycling center?" she suggested.

A relieved grin spread across Jaidon's face. "Good thinking. Okay, then. Saturday it is. We can pick you up. Dad has to make some deliveries in town."

Lola nodded eagerly. They arranged the time and she gave him her address.

The bell rang and kids started to file into school for afternoon classes. Lola, Storm, and Jaidon headed back across the playground together.

When they got into class, Lola sat down at her desk and Storm jumped onto her lap. "Can you believe it?" she whispered to him. "It looks like we're actually going to see where Jaidon lives. I never thought he'd invite me over, not after those kids at his old school were so horrible to him. He must trust me a little bit."

Storm yapped agreement. He tilted his little round head and looked up at her with a playful I-told-you-so expression.

Lola spluttered with laughter and then, as Ms. Dobson looked over at her and frowned, quickly turned it into a cough.

Friday dawned bright and clear. Lola was relaxing against the back of her seat as the bus headed toward the recycling center. Storm was leaning up out of the bag on her lap to watch the houses and stores speeding past.

Lola looked across at Jaidon, who was sitting beside her. "This beats being in class, doesn't it?" she said.

Jaidon nodded. "Sure does."

Carly, Treena, and Lee were on the bus's long backseat, directly behind them. Treena and Lee were giggling and talking in whispers. At one point, a cascade of chips came pinging over on to Lola and Jaidon.

"Idiots," Jaidon grumbled, brushing himself down. He looked pale and tense and Lola wondered if he was starting to remember what it felt like to be bullied. "Just ignore them. They'll soon get sick of messing around," she said.

Two minutes later, something landed
in her hair and Lola reached up to find
that whatever it was, it was stuck fast.

Storm gave an indignant little woof.
He leaned up, grasped the sticky candy
wrapper in his teeth and gently pulled it
out of her hair.

Lola patted him to say thanks.

It went quiet in the backseat for about two minutes and then Lola heard a sloshing sound as a can of soda was being shaken up. An arm appeared round the side of their seat and the ring pull popped, spraying soda in Jaidon's lap.

Lee peered over their seat.

"Jaidon's wet himself!" he shouted. Treena cackled with laughter. Jaidon was scarlet. He clenched his fists and looked really upset.

Lola prickled with annoyance on his behalf. Whipping round, she glared at Treena and Lee. "Why don't you two grow up?"

Lee stuck out his tongue. "Who rattled your cage? Do you want a lemonade shampoo?" He shook the can again, before taking aim.

Lola felt a familiar warm tingling sensation down her spine as bright golden sparks ignited in Storm's black-and-white fur. She shook her head at Lee slowly. "Big mistake. Huge!"

Storm raised a tiny front paw and a stream of invisible sparks shot toward Lee's can. A huge fountain of soda backfired into the backseat, to a chorus of squeals and loud yells.

Lola and Jaidon turned around and looked over their seats. Treena, Carly, and Lee sat there with drenched T-shirts and faces.

"You total idiot, Lee! Look at my hair!" Carly wailed, wringing it out with two hands.

"It wasn't my fault!" Lee cried. "It must have been a damaged can!"

The three of them started arguing.

"That showed them. Thanks, Storm," Lola said, under the cover of all the noise.

Ms. Dobson made her way to the back of the bus. "What's going on back here?" she demanded, glaring at the three sticky, soaked kids. "Carly and Treena, come to the front and sit near me."

"I didn't do anything!" Carly protested, but she got up with Treena and followed the teacher.

"That was weird," Jaidon said, looking puzzled. "It looked like about ten gallons of soda shot out of Lee's can. I don't get it."

"Beats me," Lola said innocently.

Fifteen minutes later, the coach reached the recycling center. Ms. Dobson told everyone to leave their coats and bags on the bus. "You don't need to carry anything. We'll come back here to have our lunch."

Lola realized that she wasn't going to be able to carry Storm in her book bag. "It might safer if you waited here for me," she whispered to him.

Storm's muzzle wrinkled in disappointment. "I would rather come with you. I will be careful to stay close."

"Well—okay, then," Lola said reluctantly, still not convinced that a recycling center was the right place for a lively puppy to be on the loose.

After everyone got off the bus, the manager met them. He explained that this was a "hard-hat area," and they had to wear special head protection.

Lola liked her red plastic helmet and

bright yellow coat. "This is great. I feel like a firefighter or something!"

Storm trotted along at heel, as Lola, Jaidon, and the rest of the class were taken on a tour of the center, passing big heaps of smashed cars, lines of rusty fridges and washing machines, and bins full of broken glass.

Jaidon looked across at a pile of old

tires. "My dad's seen people making shoes
out of those. He used to work in East
Africa, where they make lots of things
out of trash."

Lola was impressed. "Wow! My dad
works in a boring office all day." She felt
pleased to have someone to share stuff like
this with.

Storm had paused beside Lola. She
could tell by his twitching nose and
pricked ears that he was eager to go off
exploring. She felt sorry that the trip
wasn't turning out to be much fun for
him.

They all trooped inside to watch a
video about recycling, and Lola managed
to give her impatient little friend a cuddle
without anyone seeing. After the video,
they were allowed to split into smaller

groups and return to the bus for lunch.

Lola and Storm wandered past some
tall piles of cardboard boxes. A man
driving a forklift truck was moving the tall
stacks around. Lola spotted a rabbit sitting
on a nearby patch of grass beyond the
cardboard area.

Storm saw it at the same time. His
stocky little body froze with excitement as
he zeroed in on the little brown shape.

"Storm, don't . . . ," Lola warned.

But it was too late. After being on his

best behavior all morning, Storm couldn't resist the chance of an exciting chase. With an eager little woof, he tore toward the nearest cardboard tower, just as it wobbled. It was going to fall!

Lola gasped in horror as the stack of cardboard began toppling. Storm hadn't noticed and was almost beneath it!

Chapter
SEVEN

"Hey! Where did that puppy come from?" someone shouted.

Lola realized that, in his excitement, Storm must have forgotten to stay invisible, and now he couldn't use his magic without giving himself away.

Without a second thought, she raced forward. One step, two steps. Grab! By a complete miracle, Lola scooped Storm

up by the scruff of his neck, but she was
going too fast to stop. She fell, rolling over
and over, while still holding the puppy
safely against her body.

There was a loud thud as heavy
cardboard crashed to the ground, missing
them by inches. As Lola rose her feet,
pain shot through her right elbow, but
she ignored it and went to sit on the grass
with Storm.

"Thank you for saving me, Lola,"
Storm woofed, looking subdued as she set
him on his feet. "You were very brave."

"I'm not really. I couldn't bear
anything to happen to you," Lola said. She
winced. Now that Storm was safe, she felt
sick and shaky and her arm was hurting
like mad.

Storm's eyes widened with concern.
"You are hurt. I will make you better," he
woofed.

There were shouts of alarm and the
sound of people running toward Lola
and Storm, who were still hidden from
everyone by the collapsed cardboard tower.

Lola felt a familiar tingling sensation
as Storm huffed out a warm puppy breath
of tiny gold sparkles. The glittering mist
gently swirled around Lola's sore arm,

sinking into it, and she felt the pain fade away completely.

"Thanks, Storm. That was awesome. I'm fine now," she whispered. She stood up and walked back around the heap of cardboard. "Uh-oh," she breathed as Ms. Dobson rushed up to her.

The teacher looked pale and shaken. "You silly girl! Whatever did you think you were doing running after that stray dog? Are you hurt?"

"No. I'm . . . um . . . fine," Lola said soberly. "Sorry, ma'am."

Her heart sank as she realized that she was in serious trouble. She'd probably get double detention and extra homework for a year. But when she glanced at Storm, who stood there with his big blue eyes looking up at her, she knew that she would have done the same thing all over again.

Before everyone went home on Friday, Ms. Dobson explained that the competition would be judged on Monday. "So you have the weekend to think about bringing one final thing in to school. Try to make it something unusual. There'll be extra points for originality."

"I've already got a great idea!" Carly said, looking smug.

Lola rolled her eyes at Jaidon. "Trust her!"

He grinned back. As they shared the moment, Lola realized that she and Jaidon were actually turning out to be a pretty good team.

Unfortunately Lola had been right about the detention. She sat in the empty classroom after everyone else had left for home, finishing the extra work Ms. Dobson assigned her. Luckily, Lola had Storm with her, so she didn't feel quite so bad.

"Can you believe that she's docked points from my team as well?" Lola complained. "That's put Carly, Lee, and Treena back in the lead again."

"I am sorry that you are being punished because of me," Storm yapped.

"It's not your fault," Lola said, smiling

fondly at him. He looked so cute with his little fringe falling over his eyes. "I'm just glad you're okay. I'll make sure that you're safe here forever!"

Storm's face became very serious. "I can't stay here forever, Lola. One day I will have to return to my home world and the Moon-claw pack. I hope you understand."

"I guess so," Lola murmured, realizing that she'd never be ready to lose her little friend.

Ms. Dobson came in to tell her that she could go home. Lola packed her school books and left quickly. She decided not to think about Storm having to leave and to enjoy every single moment with him.

Lola was ready and waiting on Saturday morning, when a brightly decorated van drew up outside. The sliding door opened, and Jaidon jumped out.

"He's here! Come on, Storm!" she called.

She said her good-byes to her mom and dad, before racing downstairs and going outside. For a moment she felt embarrassed by the graffiti on the walls and the scruffy paths and lawns littered with trash.

But Jaidon greeted her with a grin and didn't seem to have noticed, so Lola pushed her worries aside. *Jaidon's not like Carly*, she reminded herself silently.

"Hi! I like your van!" Lola said, admiring the painted rainbow, swirls of leaves and sunflowers, and the big smiling sun face.

"Thanks." Jaidon smiled.

"Hello, Mr. Brooks. Pleased to meet you," Lola said politely.

"The pleasure's all mine. And call me Piper. Everyone does." Jaidon's dad had a tanned face and longish fair hair. His blue eyes crinkled when he smiled, which also revealed a chipped front tooth.

"Why do they call you that?" Lola asked, before she could stop herself. She

hoped that hadn't sounded rude.

Piper didn't mind. He fished a bamboo panpipe from his pocket and played a few lilting notes. "See? I'm a piper."

Lola climbed into the backseat and sat with her bag, with Storm inside, on her lap. Jaidon was quiet and seemed tense as they drove through the busy downtown and then headed toward the quieter roads on the outskirts. After another ten minutes, a long wall, with cast-iron gates set between stone pillars, came into view. Piper steered the van through the open gates.

Lola saw a large sign. It read:

Welcome to the Sunlight Peace Community

"I wonder why we've stopped here. Maybe Piper has to make another delivery," she whispered to Storm, remembering what Jaidon had said about his dad delivering fruit and vegetables to people.

They stopped in front of a huge redbrick house. It had an imposing stone porch and a round tower at one end. Wide paths divided the well-kept lawns and neat flower beds. Lola could see people working in the grounds; others were sitting on the grass relaxing. It looked like they all lived here.

As they got out of the van, Piper flashed Lola and Jaidon a smile. "I've things to do, so I'll see you two later." He turned to Lola. "You should feel highly honored, you know. Jaidon hasn't invited anyone home in ages." He strolled away toward the large house.

Lola turned to Jaidon. "Home? It's a joke, right? You can't live *here*?" she said, gaping in astonishment.

Jaidon's face clouded. "I knew it was a mistake to bring you here," he said in a hurt voice. "You're going to make fun of me now, just like those other kids!" Tears glinted in his eyes as he spun on his heel and marched away.

Chapter
EIGHT

"Hey! Wait!" Lola called. She hurried after Jaidon with Storm running by her side. Jaidon didn't wait for her or slow down. Lola had to walk fast to keep up with him.

"This is me, remember? I'm not making fun of anyone," she exclaimed. "All I meant was that I've been thinking that you lived on some little farm or

something. This place's awesome."

Jaidon stopped and turned to face her. "Really? You don't think I'm strange because I live in a Peace Community?"

Lola shook her head. "No! Why should I? It just makes you interesting and different. Do you care that I live in a messy neighborhood?"

"No way!" A relieved smile spread

across Jaidon's face and his shoulders slumped. "Do you want to have a look around then?"

"Of course I do!" Lola said, giving Jaidon a friendly nudge. "Tell me all about what a Peace Community is, and *don't* leave anything out."

"Okay!" Jaidon said, doing a pretend salute in response to her playful, bossy comment.

They were both laughing as they set off together. Lola noticed that Storm was craning his neck and looking hopefully toward the huge lawns. "Can we look around outside first?" she asked, knowing that her little friend must be eager for a walk.

Jaidon agreed readily. "We'll go this way toward the lake, and then I'll show

you the vegetable gardens. I've got my
own patch there."

Storm kicked up his heels and
scampered off toward the nearest tree.
They wound down paths past a grove of
trees and soon came to a beautiful, calm
lake with an island in the center. On the
shore was a wooden pagoda, painted red
and gold, where people could sit and
enjoy the view.

"Wow! It's so gorgeous here," Lola said
admiringly, thinking of the contrast to her
neighborhood. "Is this all really, like . . .
your backyard?"

"Sort of, but it's not just mine," Jaidon
explained. "Me and my mom and dad
live here at the center with lots of other
families. We have our own rooms in the
house, but we usually all eat together and

we take turns with cooking and growing our food. We sell some of our stuff, too. That's what Dad delivers to customers in his van. And there's a café, a store, and a place for prayer, which visitors who come here to enjoy the grounds can also use."

Lola was fascinated. She hadn't known places like this existed. She thought it seemed like a great way to live.

Storm was enjoying himself, too. Lola spotted him rooting about in some rushes. When he scampered back toward her, she could see that his nose and little muzzle were all muddy.

Jaidon led Lola and Storm into the garden with its rows of leafy vegetables and frames of red-flowered string beans. Other fruits and vegetables were being grown in a row of huge greenhouses.

"Do you want to see my pets?" Jaidon asked, with a gleam in his eye.

Lola nodded, wondering what they could be. Chickens, goats, or even pigs? But her eyes widened when Jaidon stopped next to a large plastic tub. Whatever could he be keeping in there?

Jaidon removed the lid with a flourish. "Meet—my worms!"

Lola fell over laughing as she peered in at the rich, crumbly compost, which the worms were busy making from kitchen and garden waste. *Trust Jaidon to have the weirdest pets on the planet!*

They had delicious strawberry smoothies and coconut pancakes in the café, where Jaidon's mom was working. Anjum Brooks had a calm oval face, glowing skin, and warm dark eyes. "I am very glad that Jaidon has a new friend. You are welcome here anytime," she said to Lola.

"Thanks!" Lola smiled, giving Storm a secret cuddle under the table. She hoped to get the chance to come here again. She was starting to think that she and Jaidon could become real friends and not just teammates.

After they finished eating, Jaidon and Lola sat in one of the Brooks family's rooms to write up their recycling report.

Storm lay on the rug by Lola's feet with his nose between his little front paws.

"I wonder what happened to that little black-and-white puppy you saved from getting hurt," Jaidon commented.

"It . . . um . . . ran away. I didn't see where it went," Lola said vaguely, trying not to look at Storm. "Sorry that we lost points because of me."

"Doesn't matter. It was just bad luck. I'd have done exactly the same thing as you."

Lola felt herself warming even more to Jaidon. Any other kid would have been mad at her for losing their team points.

She looked up from her notes and chewed the end of her pen thoughtfully.

"We're supposed to be taking some really unusual recycled object to school on Monday, aren't we?" she remembered. "Ms. Dobson's giving out extra points for originality."

Storm sat up and scratched himself with one short little back leg. His ears swiveled as he listened.

"We definitely need those points, or Carly's team's going to win easily," Jaidon said with a sigh. "But I haven't got any more bright ideas."

Storm jumped to his feet. "Follow me, Lola!" he yapped excitedly, jumping up and padding toward the door.

Lola wasn't sure what Storm had in mind, but she nodded. "I might . . .

er . . . have an idea. Come on!" she said to Jaidon, hurrying after the puppy.

They retraced their steps into the garden.

"So—what are we doing here?" Jaidon asked when they were standing next to the plastic-tub worm factory.

"Um . . . I'm just thinking it through," Lola said, playing for time. She glanced at Storm for help, but he was sitting on the

garden path, wagging his tail and saying nothing.

Lola realized that her fluffy friend wanted her to work this out for herself. She lifted the lid again and looked inside the plastic tub. *Worms—garbage—compost.* An idea flashed into her mind. "That's it! You're awesome, Stor– I mean, er . . . I'm awesome!" she burst out, turning to Jaidon.

"I know what we can take into class!" she said triumphantly.

Chapter
NINE

Lola took Storm outside for a walk
before she went to bed Sunday night.
The field behind her apartment block had
been mown earlier that day, and the fresh
smell of cut grass filled the air.

"Thanks for helping me decide what
to take to school," she said to Storm.

"You are welcome." Storm snuffled
about in the short grass.

Suddenly, Lola heard fierce barking
and growling coming from over near the
garages. Storm stiffened and began to
tremble all over.

"What's wrong?" she asked softly.

"Shadow knows I am here. He has
used his magic to make any dogs that are
nearby my enemies!" Storm whimpered.

He gave a whine of terror and dashed under the slide in the nearby kids' playground.

Lola thought the growling was getting fainter. She could see a woman grappling with two Labradors that had spotted a squirrel sitting in a tree. As she watched, the woman got the dogs under control and walked away across the field.

Lola got down and went to peer under the slide. She could see Storm there, curled into a tiny ball.

"Those dogs have gone now. I don't think they were here for you. But how will I recognize any that are?"

Storm lifted his head. "They will have fierce pale eyes and extra-long teeth," he told her.

"Then we'll have to hide you extra

well," Lola said. She managed to reach right underneath the slide with one arm and stroke Storm reassuringly.

The terrified puppy slowly uncurled and finally crawled out with his belly low to the grass. Lola picked him up. She could feel his heart beating wildly. "You're safe for now. I hope that horrible Shadow keeps going to the other side of the world!"

Storm looked up at her, his squashed little face serious. "He is very close, Lola. I can sense it. If he comes for me, I may have to leave suddenly, without saying good-bye."

Lola felt a pang as she was reminded that Storm couldn't stay with her forever. But she didn't want to think about that now. She loved having Storm all to herself.

"Come on, let's go inside. You've had a nasty shock," she crooned. Lola and Storm met up with Jaidon in the playground on Monday morning. There had been no more sign of any fierce dogs, and Storm was back to his normal self.

"Did you bring it?" Lola asked eagerly.

Jaidon nodded. He produced a clear plastic box. "Mom found this to put it in. It used to have soap inside."

They went into class where lots of kids were already milling round the display table and talking about what they'd brought in. There was an air of excitement. Everyone wanted to win the prize.

Ms. Dobson came in and took attendance and then walked over to the display table. "Now, class, I hope you've all

brought in something special. I'm going to be looking for the most unusual recycled object, remember?"

Kids had brought in pens, letter-writing sets, and reusable shopping bags. Carly proudly produced a drinking glass made from an old bottle. She smirked, obviously assuming that this was the wining object.

"Very good, everyone," the teacher praised.

Lola had waited until last. She and Jaidon put the plastic container on the counter and opened the lid. Inside there was something that looked like crumbled chocolate brownies.

"They've brought in a cow pie! Ugh! That's gross!" cried Carly.

The other kids crowded close. Some of them were wrinkling their noses and giggling. "It's only compost. Don't you know anything?" Jaidon scoffed.

Carly flushed, not used to Jaidon standing up for himself. "Well, it's still disgusting! You'll probably get disqualified from the comp."

"I don't think so, Carly." Ms. Dobson had a big smile on her face. "That's excellent, Jaidon and Lola. We couldn't have a better example of recycling in action. Fruit and vegetable waste gets turned into compost by worms and other creatures in the soil, and then the compost can be used for growing things. Nothing is wasted."

Lola beamed at Jaidon as the teacher looked at all the other items. Then everyone crowded around as Ms. Dobson added points to the wall chart. The girl with the pens got four, the boy with the reusable bag got five, and Carly got six points for her glass.

"And finally, ten points go to—Lola and Jaidon!"

"Yay! We've done it!" Lola waved her arms in the air. She grabbed Jaidon and they danced around in victory.

Everyone clapped and cheered. Even Carly's teammates left her sulking in the corner to give Lola and Jaidon a round of applause.

As the noise died down, Lola looked about for Storm, wanting to include him in the celebrations. Just then, the tiny puppy gave a whimper of fear and tore out of the open classroom door. Lola glimpsed sinister dark shapes running across the playing field toward the classroom. Sunlight glinted on their cold, pale eyes and extra-long teeth.

She gasped. Shadow's dogs! Storm was in terrible danger. The moment she had been dreading was here—and far more quickly than she ever could have expected.

Her heart pounded as she knew she was going to have to be strong for Storm's sake.

"I've got to grab something!" Lola said hastily to Jaidon, as she dashed out

of the classroom. She ran down the
corridor and had just rushed into the
coat room when a dazzling flash of
bright gold light lit up the racks of coats
and lockers.

"Oh!" she gasped, rubbing her eyes.
Storm stood there, looking magnificent
as his powerful true self. Gold sparkles
glittered in his thick silver-gray neck-
ruff and his eyes glowed like sapphires.
An adult wolf with a gentle face and
wise golden eyes stood next to Storm.

Tears ached in Lola's throat. "Your
enemies are here! Save yourself, Storm!"
she burst out.

Storm's glowing midnight blue eyes
narrowed with affection. "You have
been a good friend, Lola. Be of good
heart," he said in a velvety growl.

Biting back a sob, Lola ran forward and threw her arms round Storm's muscular neck. She breathed in the smell of his rain-scented fur. "I'm really going to miss you, Storm. I'll never forget you," she whispered, her voice breaking.

He allowed her to hug him one last time and then stepped backward.

There was a final flash and a silent explosion of big gold sparks that showered down around Lola like warm rain and crackled as they hit the floor. Storm and his mother faded and were gone.

A furious snarling sounded from outside, but then all was silent.

Lola stood there, stunned by how fast it had all happened, but she was glad that she'd had a chance to say good-bye to her magical friend. She knew that she would always remember the special time she had spent with Storm, and he would be her secret forever.

She looked round with tears in her eyes to see Jaidon standing there.

"Lola! There you are! Ms. Dobson sent me to find you. She's going to give out the prize. Are you okay?" he asked, frowning slightly. "If you're worried about something you can . . . um . . . always tell me."

"Thanks, but I'm fine. I was just coming!" Lola took a deep breath as she walked back toward the classroom with her new friend. She was really looking forward to sharing the movie tickets and asking her mom and dad if Jaidon could come to visit afterward. She knew that wherever Storm was now, the magic puppy would be proud of them both.

About the
AUTHOR

Sue Bentley's books for children often
include animals, fairies, and wildlife. She
lives in Northampton, England, and enjoys
reading, going to the movies, relaxing
by her garden pond, and watching the
birds feeding their babies on the lawn.
At school she was always getting yelled
at for daydreaming or staring out of the
window—but she now realizes that she
was storing up ideas for when she became
a writer. She has met and owned many
cats and dogs, and each one has brought a
special kind of magic to her life.

Don't miss these Magic Puppy books!

Don't miss these Magic Kitten books!

Don't miss these Magic Ponies books!

#1 A New Friend

#2 A Special Wish

#3 A Twinkle of Hooves

#4 Show-Jumping Dreams

#5 Winter Wonderland

#6 Riding Rescue

#7 Circus Surprise

#8 Pony Camp

Don't miss these Magic Bunny books!